The Three Little Pigs

A Puffin Easy-to-Read Classic

retold by Harriet Ziefert

illustrated by Laura Rader

PUFFIN BOOKS

PUFFIN BOOKS
Published by the Penguin Group
Penguin Putnam Books for Young Readers,
345 Hudson Street, New York, New York 10014, U.S.A.
Penguin Books Ltd, 80 Strand, London WC2R ORL, England
Penguin Books Australia Ltd, 250 Camberwell Road, Camberwell, Victoria 3124, Australia
Penguin Books Canada Ltd, 20 Alcorn Avenue, Toronto, Ontario, Canada M4V 3B2
Penguin Books (N.Z.) Ltd, 282-290 Wairau Road, Auckland 20, New Zealand

Penguin Books Ltd, Registered Offices: Harmondsworth, Middlesex, England

First published in the United States of America by Viking, a division of Penguin Books USA Inc., 1995
Published simultaneously by Puffin Books, a division of Penguin Putnam Books for Young Readers, 1995

17   19   20   18

THE LIBRARY OF CONGRESS HAS CATALOGED THE VIKING EDITION AS FOLLOWS:
Ziefert, Harriet.
The three little pigs / Harriet Ziefert; illustrated by Laura Rader.
p. cm. –(Viking easy-to-read)
Summary: Three little pigs leave home to seek their fortunes and have to deal with a threatening wolf.
ISBN-0-670-86051-4
[1. Folklore. 2. Pigs—Folklore.] I. Rader, Laura, ill. II. Title. III. Series.
PZ8.1.Z55Th   1995   398.24'529734—dc20   [E]   94-43073   CIP   AC

Puffin Easy-to-Read ISBN 0-14-037624-0
Printed in the United States of America
Puffin® and Easy-to-Read® are registered trademarks of Penguin Putnam Inc.

Reading Level 1.9

The Three Little Pigs

Three little pigs
went out into the world.

The first little pig met
a man carrying straw.

The little pig asked,
"May I have some straw
so I can build a house?"

"Yes," said the man.
"You can have some straw."

The first little pig
took the straw.
He built a straw house.

A wolf came along and
knocked on the door.
"Little pig, little pig,
let me come in."

"Not by the hair
of my chinny, chin, chin!"
said the little pig.

"Then I'll huff,
and I'll puff,
and I'll blow your house in,"
said the wolf.

And he huffed.
And he puffed.
And he blew the house in.
And he ate up the first little pig.

The second little pig
met a man carrying sticks.

The little pig asked,
"May I have some sticks
so I can build a house?"

"Yes," said the man.
"You can have some sticks."

The second little pig
took the sticks.

He built
a stick house.

A wolf came along and
knocked on the door.
"Little pig, little pig,
let me come in."

"Not by the hair
of my chinny, chin, chin!"
said the little pig.

"Then I'll huff,
and I'll puff,
and I'll blow your house in,"
said the wolf.

And he huffed.
And he puffed.
And he blew the house in.

And he ate up the second little pig.

The third little pig met
a man carrying bricks.

The little pig asked,
"May I have some bricks
so I can build a house?"

"Yes," said the man.
"You can have some bricks."

The third little pig
took the bricks.

He built a brick house.

A wolf came along and
knocked on the door.
"Little pig, little pig,
let me come in."

"Not by the hair
of my chinny, chin, chin!"
said the little pig.

"Then I'll huff,
and I'll puff,
and I'll blow your house in,"
said the wolf.

And he huffed, and he puffed.
And he huffed, and he puffed.
He could not blow the brick house in.

The wolf was angry.
He jumped on the roof.
He yelled, "Little pig,
I'm coming down the chimney.
I'm going to eat you up!"

But the little pig was smart.
He was smarter than the wolf.
He had a big pot of hot water
in the fireplace.

The little pig lifted the cover.
The wolf fell into the pot.

The little pig lived happily
in his little brick house.